*To Miranda, Colin, and Evan—*s.s.w.

*To my parents, and Pope Innocent XII—*e.d.

ACKNOWLEDGMENTS

I am grateful to several experts who assisted in my preparation of the text. I especially wish to thank Dr. Paul Johnson, chairman of the department of entomology, University of New Hampshire, who offered valuable suggestions, read the completed text, and checked it for accuracy.

I also thank the following individuals: Don Salvatore of the Museum of Science, Boston, Massachusetts, who discussed this project with me and provided anecdotes of insect behavior; and Dr. Karolis Bagdonis of the University of Wyoming, who provided information about the rare Prairie Sphinx Moth.

10 9 8 7 6 5 4 3 2 1

Library of Congress Cataloging-in-Publication Data: Whayne, Susanne Santoro. The world of insects / by Susanne Santoro Whayne ; illustrated by Ebet Dudley. p. cm. Summary: Describes the life cycles, physical characteristics, and behavior of a variety of insects, including the swallowtail butterfly, ant, cricket, and mayfly. ISBN 0-671-69018-3 1. Insects—Juvenile literature. [1. Insects.] I. Dudley, Ebet, ill. II. Title. QL467.2.W44 1990
595.7—dc20   89-28305

THE WORLD OF INSECTS

By Susanne Santoro Whayne
Illustrated by Ebet Dudley

SIMON AND SCHUSTER BOOKS FOR YOUNG READERS
Published by Simon & Schuster Inc.
New York • London • Toronto • Sydney • Tokyo • Singapore

A World Full of Insects

At any time of the day or night, you can see insects going about their business. At dawn, a ladybug crosses a leaf in search of breakfast. In the noon sunlight, butterflies flutter across a field. At twilight, the night shift takes over. Fireflies signal to each other on the lawn; moths visit our screens; at midnight, a mosquito awakens us with its buzz.

Wherever you go, from tropical rain forests to the Arctic Circle, you will find insects. They can walk on water, like the delicate water strider, or live *in* it, like the young mayfly. Insects have even been found cruising more than three miles aboveground!

Insects have flourished on the Earth from the earliest times. They were among the first creatures to leave the water for a life on land, and the very first to take to the air. Two hundred million years ago, huge dragonflies the size of hawks buzzed through the forest.

Today, nine out of every ten living creatures are insects. Their huge numbers make them the most successful creatures ever to live on the Earth. At least 1½ million different kinds of insects have been identified, more than all the species of animals and plants put together. And hundreds of thousands of insects have yet to be named. *Entomologists*, people who study insects, believe at least 4 million species of insects may live on the Earth today.

Secrets of Success

What are the secrets of the insects' success? Their small size for one. Tiny creatures grow and reproduce very rapidly. On a good day a termite queen can lay 30,000 eggs. An elephant, on the other hand, needs almost two years to produce just one baby. Small insects also require less food to survive. Think of how much a St. Bernard eats in one day, then consider how little a flea needs!

An insect is built for successful protection and movement. A tough outer shell, called an *exoskeleton*, covers much of its body. This is actually its skeleton, worn on the outside. Wings attached to their *thorax*, or chest area, give many insects tremendous speed to hunt their prey and escape from enemies. At twenty MPH a dragonfly could keep up with your bicycle!

Also attached to an insect's thorax are six legs—no more, no less. (A spider with eight legs may look like an insect, but it is not.) Wingless insects rely on their powerful leg muscles. A flea can jump 130 times its own height. If you had that ability, you could leap over the Washington Monument!

Some insects are neither strong fliers nor powerful jumpers. Their success depends on their ability to hide from their enemies. This Sphinx moth is almost impossible to pick out from tree bark. And can you find the walking stick among the leaves?

Insects owe much of their success to their sharp senses. Their antennae are used for smelling, often their most important sense, as well as for hearing. These antennae are so keen that some male moths can smell a female three miles away. Insects can also sense in weird yet practical ways. Can you guess why it's useful for a butterfly to taste with its feet?

Sight is also important to insects, although they see the world differently than we do. Their eyes, called *compound eyes*, are made up of many little lenses. Each lens sees a small, separate picture; and the insect's brain puts these pictures together, like pieces of a puzzle.

Perhaps the strangest reason for insect success is the way insects change as they grow older. Imagine that you began your life as a fish. Then, in junior high you became a bear cub and settled in for a long *hibernation*, or winter sleep. When you emerged from your cave, you found you were no longer a land creature, but with beautiful wings, you enjoyed the rest of your adult life as a bird! Such changes in the insect's form are called *metamorphosis*.

Changes like these are very helpful to insects. Young insects can eat their own kinds of food without competing with adults. The hibernating insects can survive for long periods of time in a protected state. And the adults can concentrate on grown-up matters like mating and egg production.

Metamorphosis

The Black Swallowtail butterfly's journey to adulthood begins in the spring, when the female lays her honey-colored eggs on the leaf of a wild carrot. Over the next ten days, the eggs darken. When an egg is quite black, a *larva* hatches. For butterflies and moths, the larval form is called a *caterpillar*. His first meal is his eggshell; and after he finishes that, he has plenty of carrot leaves to eat.

Since they can't move very fast, caterpillars need built-in protection. Many have sharp spines. Some have terrible tastes or smells. Others, like the swallowtail, have a misleading appearance. The young larva resembles a very unappetizing bird dropping. Later, as he grows and sheds his skin several times, his body becomes green-and-black-striped to blend in with the surrounding leaves.

After a month or two of almost constant eating, the swallowtail caterpillar is a full-grown two inches long. Now he is ready for the next stage of his life. He spins a silk thread to hold his body to a twig. Then, as he shakes his body, his skin begins to split from top to bottom. Finally, the old skin falls away and our caterpillar has a completely new identity. He is now called a *pupa*. He will spend the next several weeks in hiding in a shell called a *chrysalis*, which will form when his outer skin hardens. The pupae of other insects, like

butterflies and some ants, spin themselves a silken hideout called a *cocoon*.

In good weather, the swallowtail pupa will spend one to four weeks in its chrysalis. If the chrysalis is formed in the autumn, the pupa will be safe inside for up to six months of winter.

On the outside, the chrysalis is quiet and still. But inside, magical changes are taking place. When the chrysalis finally breaks open, the childhood caterpillar has vanished and the adult butterfly appears.

For half an hour, the wet, crumpled swallowtail clings to his twig as his wings unfold and dry in the sun. Then, off he flies, his metamorphosis complete.

The newborn swallowtail butterfly will lead a solitary life. Except for a brief mating to fertilize eggs, he will spend the rest of his days alone among the field flowers. But in the ground below live very different insects. These are the ants, and they are so social that an individual ant cannot survive on its own.

The Ant Colony

In many ways the lives of ants are like our own. Their homes are huge cities, where hardworking inhabitants care for their young, do their housework, and bury their dead. Some ants hunt for meat, keep "livestock," and harvest grain. But ants share our more unpleasant habits, too. They go to war, keep slaves, and even burglarize other nests!

At the heart of the colony, the queen is busy laying eggs. Most of her larvae will develop into female worker ants. Surrounding the queen are nursery workers who feed the young larvae. During the day, the pampered young are moved to chambers closer to the warm surface. Cleanliness is very important to the colony. The workers groom the queen and larvae, remove debris, and bury the dead in special locations. They groom themselves, too, with little brushes on their front legs called *strigils*.

Outside the colony, workers hunt for food. When a food scout finds a morsel, she hurries back to the nest, dragging her abdomen on the ground to leave a scent trail. She catches the attention of fellow workers by excitedly tapping them with her antennae. Following the scent trail, the workers rush off before the find is spotted by a rival colony. Bringing it back is no problem—ants can carry up to forty times their own weight.

Some eggs are fed a special, protein-rich diet and develop into soldier ants. These fierce workers guard the nest, often by simply plugging up the entrance with their oversized heads. They are a terrible sight on the battlefield, where, if necessary, they will fight to the death.

Ant battles, sometimes lasting up to sixteen hours, end with victorious soldier ants using their huge jaws, called *mandibles*, to slice up their fallen enemies.

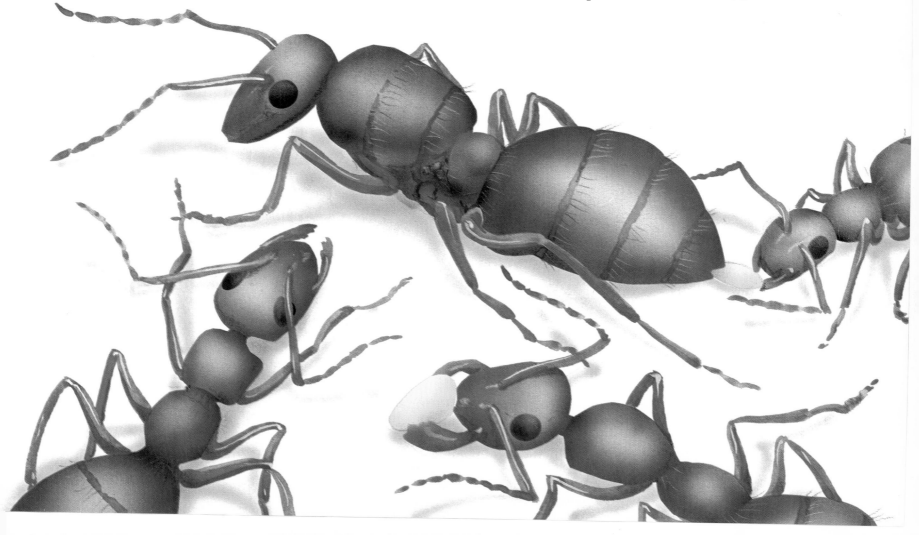

The Honeybee

For all of its life, an ant keeps to just one job, the one to which it was born. But there's no dull routine for another colony insect, the honeybee. As these workers grow and change, their jobs do, too. Variety, not long life, is a honeybee's reward, for a worker lives just six weeks.

For the first two days of her adult life, the female worker bee cannot feed herself. Like a baby bird, she begs for food by sticking out her tongue; which is called a *proboscis*. Still, there is work to do—her first job is to clean the hive.

By her third day, the young worker can help herself to the hive's honey and protein-rich pollen. As soon as she develops special glands to produce "bee milk," the worker begins nursemaid duties, feeding the larvae.

During the next three weeks, the honeybee's "milk" glands shrink, and wax-making glands appear. Our former nursery worker is now on construction duty, building and repairing the hive. But soon, she moves to food production. She receives pollen and nectar from the field bees. Then, working the nectar with her mouth, she evaporates the water and adds digestive juices to turn it into honey, which is stored in a honeycomb.

The worker is also on duty at the hive's entrance. Her keen sense of smell determines "friend or foe." In hot weather, she helps cool the hive by beating her wings like a fan.

In the last two weeks of her life, the middle-aged honeybee finally becomes a full-time worker. At each flower, she sucks up nectar with her long tongue, then stores it inside her body for the trip back to the hive. To collect a single load of nectar, a bee may visit hundreds of flowers. To produce just one pound of honey requires 40,000 bee loads of nectar. Since the hive will need about fifty pounds a year, the workers will need to carry two million bee loads back to the hive!

Gathering pollen is a little easier. Each full load of pollen requires a mere 100 flower stops for the field bee. The field worker collects the pollen with her front legs, then passes it to "pollen baskets," little openings on her rear legs.

When a worker discovers a rich field of blossoms, she shows the hive its location by a kind of dance. She crawls onto the honeycomb and uses her body like the needle of a compass. If the flowers are located straight toward the sun, she runs straight up the comb, wiggling her tail. If the field is just to the right of the sun, she wiggles slightly to the right. The farther away the flowers are, the faster the bee wiggles.

The real purpose of all this bee activity, of course, is feeding the hive for the winter. But the next time you spread a teaspoon of honey over your toast, you might want to thank a honeybee for the 2,000 bee loads of nectar it took to produce it!

The Bumblebee

As soon as the sun melts the last of the snow, a queen bumblebee emerges from her hibernation inside an old log and searches for a new summer home. An abandoned mousehole looks just right, and the queen gets busy. She makes a little cup out of her wax and dusts the bottom with pollen. After laying her eggs, she seals the cup with wax. Then, to protect her eggs, she sits on them like a mother hen.

Unlike honeybees, who spend the cold months clustered tightly around their honeycomb, only the queen bumblebee survives the winter. Her colony will be born, develop, and die out in just a few months. Since there is so much to do and so little time, bumblebees are put to work at an early age. There is no four-week honeybee training period for these young workers. Bumblebees just two days old work full time gathering pollen and nectar. And there is no pampered egg-laying existence for this queen; she often joins the field workers on their foraging trips. Into the twilight, long after the honeybees have retired to their hives for the evening, you may see a bumblebee visiting flowers.

At the end of summer, the queen stops laying worker eggs and begins to hatch queens and *drones*, the males who will mate with young queens. Without workers to clean and repair it, the nest becomes neglected and untidy. As autumn approaches, the field workers slow down and are finally overtaken by old age. Soon, the old queen undergoes a speeded-up aging. In just a few weeks, she loses her soft body hair, her golden color fades, and she can no longer lay eggs. With the first cold weather, she too will die of old age. But tucked away in a sheltered spot the new, young queens fall into a winter sleep. In the spring they will wake and, without memory or teacher, begin the work of building new colonies.

Music on Your Lawn

CRICKETS

On a summer evening, the air is filled with the sounds of many insects. Like a crowd of excited foreign travelers, they are calling to each other in their own languages. Above all the buzzes, hums, and clicks, one sound is most familiar—the chirp of the male field cricket. He is singing to his mate, telling her where he is and who he is, for each species of cricket has its own song. Their courtship call is even more amazing when you consider that he has no vocal chords and she has no ears.

How does their private concert work? He sings with his wings, and she listens with her knees! Underneath each of the male's wings is a row of little ridges and a sharp-edged scraper. To chirp, he rubs his wings together, and the scraper moves against the ridges like a bow on a fiddle's strings. His female audience picks up this sound with her "ear drums," located on her front legs, just below her knee joints.

GRASSHOPPERS

The cricket is a night musician; the grasshopper sings his songs during the heat of the day. He produces his chattering calls to his mate by rubbing his back legs against his wings.

You can recognize a female grasshopper or cricket by the long, slender tube at the end of her body. This is her *ovipositor*. She uses it to poke holes in the ground to lay her eggs in. Once young crickets and grasshoppers hatch, they are on their own. They look like miniature adults, for they do not go through a complete metamorphosis. Instead, they simply continue to grow and, from time to time, shed their skins like snakes do.

Grasshoppers have huge appetites. Short-horned grasshoppers, known as "locusts," are especially destructive to crops. But they in turn have their enemies, especially birds and ants. If you've ever surprised a grasshopper, you've seen one of his defenses, a quick jump. Although he can also fly, leaping is his specialty. He can jump twenty times his length. If you could do that, you could stand on home plate and jump past first base!

KATYDID

A katydid is a long-horned grasshopper. His horns, which are actually his antennae, are as long as his body.

The male makes his *katy-did katy-she-did* sound with his wings, like a cricket. He turns the volume up with a "sound amplifier" located on the base of each wing. It is very effective, for a female can hear his song a mile away. And just as with the female cricket, it's music to her knees!

Beetles

There are more varieties of beetles than any other kind of insect. So far more than 300,000 species have been named. As you might expect in any big family, its members can be very different. Beetles have their useful, productive family members, like the ladybug, but also their black sheep, like the destructive Japanese beetle.

Some beetles are ordinary leaf-eaters while others are record setters of many kinds. The world's heaviest insect is the African Goliath beetle, a quarter-pounder. The splendor beetle is the longest-living insect. Its larva may take thirty years to complete its metamorphosis. The champion weight lifter in the family is the scarab beetle. It can carry 850 times its own weight. If you could do that, you could pick up a stack of twenty-seven automobiles!

STAG BEETLE

The huge mandibles of the stag beetle are notched at the ends like a deer's antlers. And like stags, these beetles will fight over mates and territory. If you find a stag beetle, keep in mind that some beetles are biters. If you pick one up, you may appreciate the stag's other name, the "pinching bug"!

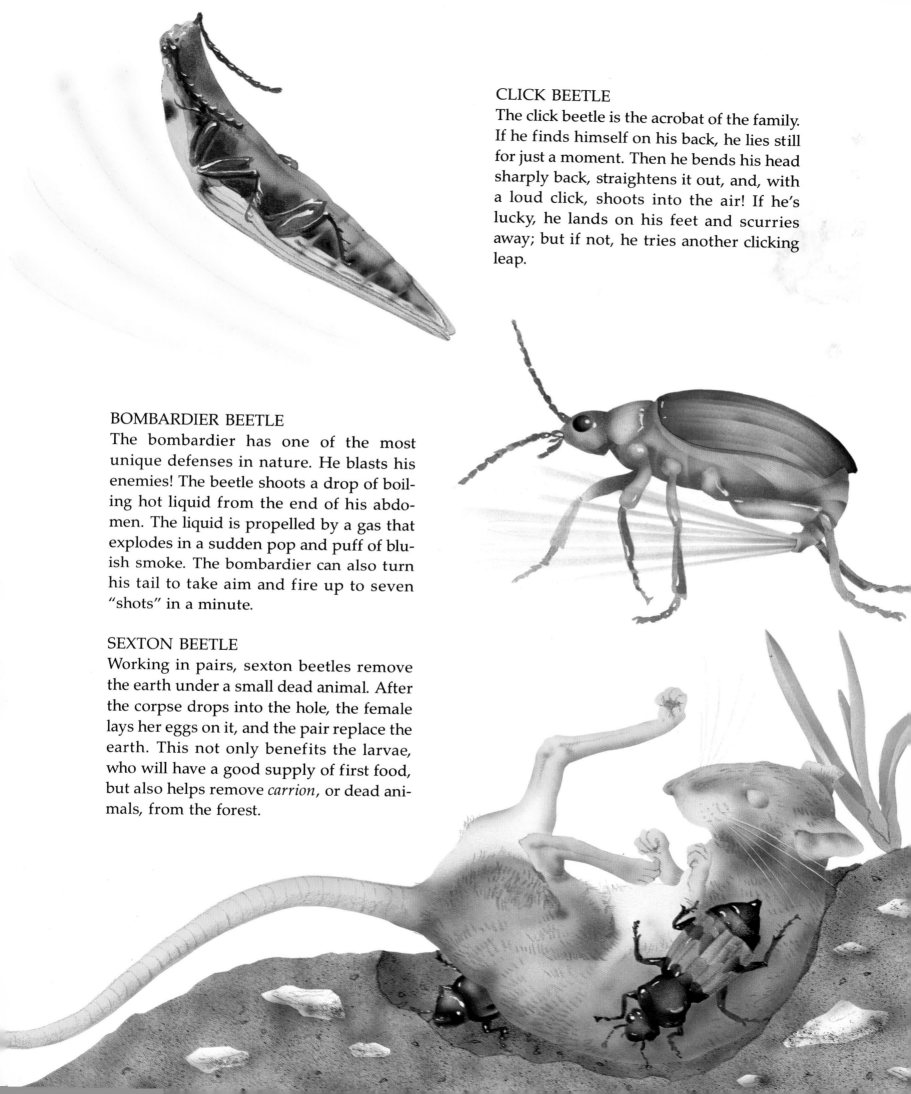

CLICK BEETLE

The click beetle is the acrobat of the family. If he finds himself on his back, he lies still for just a moment. Then he bends his head sharply back, straightens it out, and, with a loud click, shoots into the air! If he's lucky, he lands on his feet and scurries away; but if not, he tries another clicking leap.

BOMBARDIER BEETLE

The bombardier has one of the most unique defenses in nature. He blasts his enemies! The beetle shoots a drop of boiling hot liquid from the end of his abdomen. The liquid is propelled by a gas that explodes in a sudden pop and puff of bluish smoke. The bombardier can also turn his tail to take aim and fire up to seven "shots" in a minute.

SEXTON BEETLE

Working in pairs, sexton beetles remove the earth under a small dead animal. After the corpse drops into the hole, the female lays her eggs on it, and the pair replace the earth. This not only benefits the larvae, who will have a good supply of first food, but also helps remove *carrion*, or dead animals, from the forest.

SCARAB BEETLE

Pushing with her back legs, the inch-long female scarab beetle rolls a piece of dung until it's a ball the size of an orange. Using her head as a shovel, she digs a hole, pushes the ball in, then lays her eggs in it. After she covers up the dung, her eggs will have a safe hatching place—and the barnyard will be a little cleaner.

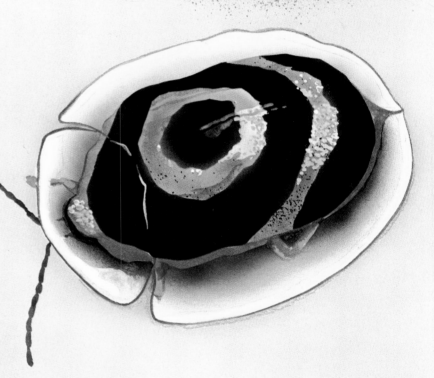

TORTOISE BEETLES

Like turtles, the tortoise beetles use their shells to hide in. They lie flat, tuck their head down, and draw in their antennae. Their beautiful red, gold, and iridescent coloring make them one of the prettiest insects.

BOLITOTHERUS BEETLE

Could this be the ugliest insect? His tough shell, covered with warty bumps, provides camouflage among the forest fungi, where he makes his home. The Bolitotherus, also known as the "Forked Fungus beetle," will eat almost anything, from seeds to decaying plants.

FIREFLIES

On a still summer night, tiny dancing lights appear on lawns and in fields. The brightest lights belong to male fireflies who hover in the air. The females answer from the ground. What looks like random flashing is actually a code for fireflies to find a mate. Each species has its own pattern, and the males and females know each other by the length of their flashes.

The firefly you see at midsummer is the very last stage of a beetle who has spent a year or two as a glowing underground larva. The adult will live just a few weeks—long enough to find a mate and produce the eggs that will carry the tiny torches for future summers.

LADYBUGS

The friendly ladybug is a welcome sight in any garden. She will confidently stroll across your hand, if you like, but after a short visit will return to her business—eating. Ladybugs have huge appetites; and, fortunately for us, their favorite meals are garden pests—aphids, mealybugs, and scale insects. In her lifetime the ladybug can rid your garden of 1,000 or more of these pests.

The ladybug's preference for aphids often puts her at odds with ants, who are quick to protect their "dairy cattle." A ladybug under siege will pull into her shell, squirt a bitter orange fluid from her leg joints, and hope for the best.

In the summer, you will usually see ladybugs alone on their leaves. But in the winter, they become quite social. Hundreds of these beetles will dig themselves into the ground around trees and spend the cold months clustered tightly together.

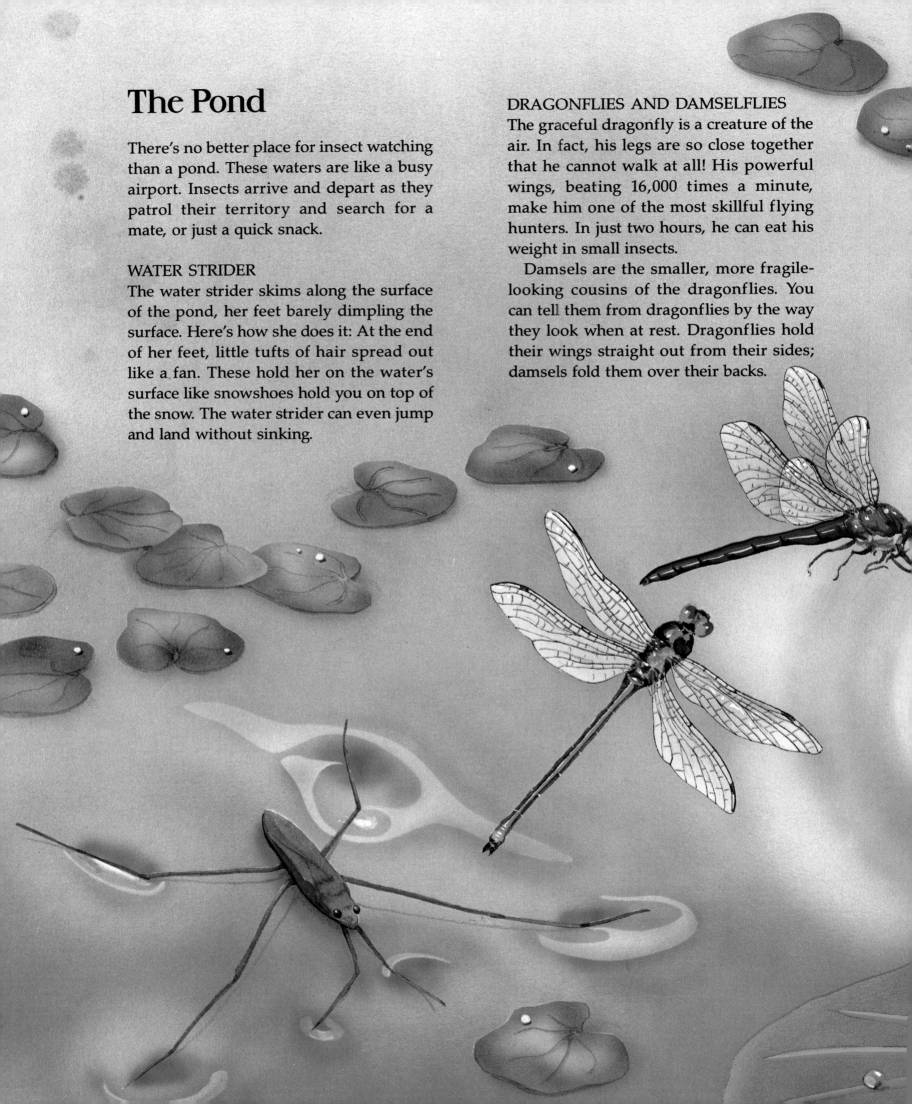

The Pond

There's no better place for insect watching than a pond. These waters are like a busy airport. Insects arrive and depart as they patrol their territory and search for a mate, or just a quick snack.

WATER STRIDER

The water strider skims along the surface of the pond, her feet barely dimpling the surface. Here's how she does it: At the end of her feet, little tufts of hair spread out like a fan. These hold her on the water's surface like snowshoes hold you on top of the snow. The water strider can even jump and land without sinking.

DRAGONFLIES AND DAMSELFLIES

The graceful dragonfly is a creature of the air. In fact, his legs are so close together that he cannot walk at all! His powerful wings, beating 16,000 times a minute, make him one of the most skillful flying hunters. In just two hours, he can eat his weight in small insects.

Damsels are the smaller, more fragile-looking cousins of the dragonflies. You can tell them from dragonflies by the way they look when at rest. Dragonflies hold their wings straight out from their sides; damsels fold them over their backs.

WHIRLIGIG BEETLES

Do they ever get dizzy? Whirligig beetles escape by spinning in circles. Although they can fly and dive, these beetles spend most of their adult life on the water's surface. To see both above and below the surface, they have divided eyes. The upper half looks up into the air, and the lower half looks down into the water. These tiny dervishes use their long, outstretched antennae to sense the tiniest ripple on the water—which is why whirligigs never seem to bump into each other.

MAYFLIES

A cloud of mayflies rises over the pond. Their swarming begins one of the shortest adulthoods in the insect world. They may mate, lay eggs, and die in only a day. In such a brief life, eating is not important; in fact, the adult mayfly has no working mouth parts.

To see more, let's look deeper—at life in the underwater pond.

The Underwater Pond

NYMPHS

This brush-tailed swimmer is a mayfly. He is so well suited for the water that he breathes through gills, like a fish. He is called a *nymph*, a name given to young insects that do not go through complete metamorphosis. Instead, over one to three years, the nymph grows and sheds his skin. When fully grown, mayfly nymphs float to the surface and, after a final molting, enjoy their few hours of adulthood.

Dragonfly nymphs breathe and move like squid, taking in water, then pushing it out in a kind of jet propulsion. Nymphs are very useful to ponds, as food for trout and as hearty eaters of mosquito larvae.

Like mayflies, damselfly nymphs breathe through gills. In the spring, the fully grown nymph climbs up the stems of a water plant and sheds her exoskeleton one last time. As she flies off to her new life in the air, she leaves behind her old shell, still clinging to the water reed like a cellophane shadow.

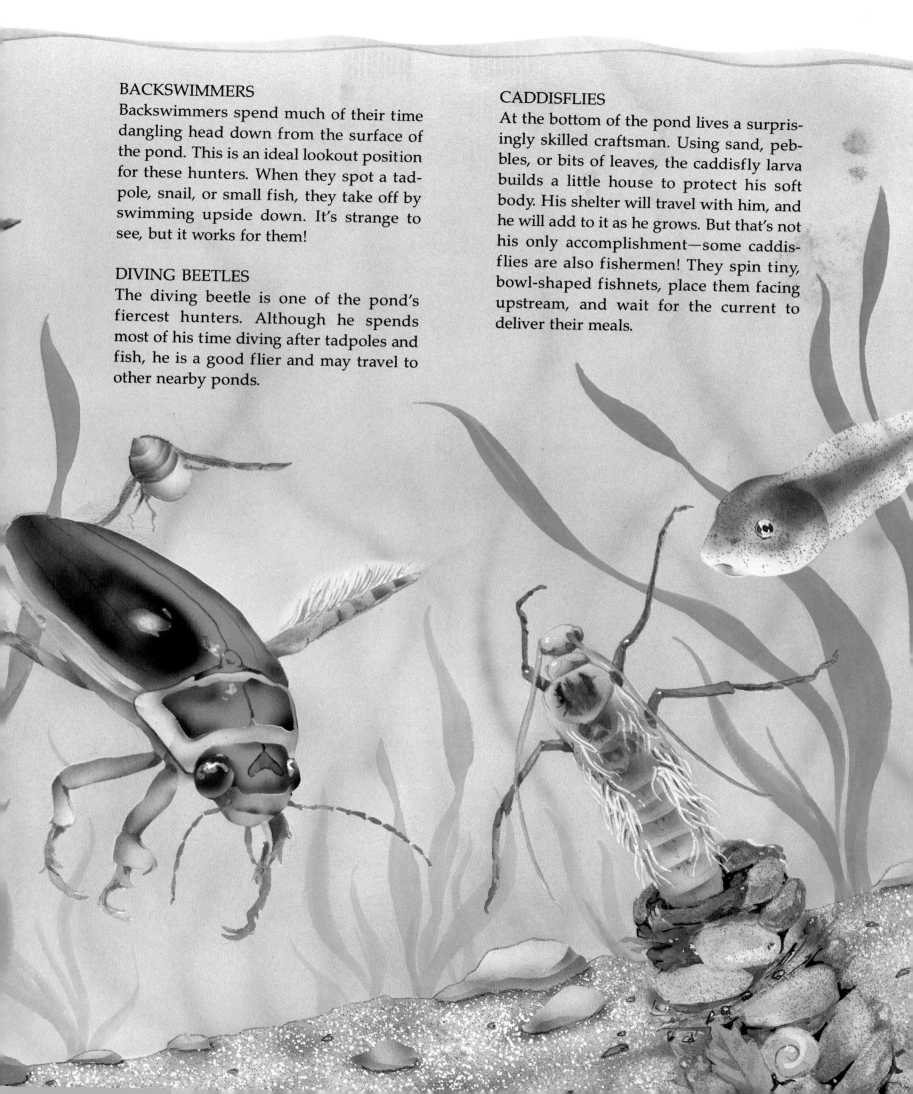

BACKSWIMMERS

Backswimmers spend much of their time dangling head down from the surface of the pond. This is an ideal lookout position for these hunters. When they spot a tadpole, snail, or small fish, they take off by swimming upside down. It's strange to see, but it works for them!

DIVING BEETLES

The diving beetle is one of the pond's fiercest hunters. Although he spends most of his time diving after tadpoles and fish, he is a good flier and may travel to other nearby ponds.

CADDISFLIES

At the bottom of the pond lives a surprisingly skilled craftsman. Using sand, pebbles, or bits of leaves, the caddisfly larva builds a little house to protect his soft body. His shelter will travel with him, and he will add to it as he grows. But that's not his only accomplishment—some caddisflies are also fishermen! They spin tiny, bowl-shaped fishnets, place them facing upstream, and wait for the current to deliver their meals.

Butterflies of the United States

If an insect popularity contest were held, butterflies would probably be the winners. The dazzling colors and designs of butterflies and moths are created by thousands of tiny, overlapping scales on their wings. The Latin name for this group of insects is Lepidoptera, which comes from the Greek words for "scale" and "wings."

MOURNING CLOAK

The Mourning Cloak is one of the first butterflies of spring. The adults hibernate over the winter and wake up as the last snow is melting. You can see them in the fields and woods of eastern Canada and the United States.

SWALLOWTAILS

The wings of most swallowtails end in the long "tails" that give them their names. The Giant Swallowtails, with wingspans of up to 5½ inches, are the largest of American butterflies. Like all swallowtails, they are strong fliers. Look for them on flowers from Massachusetts to Florida, and west to Minnesota.

GREAT PURPLE HAIRSTREAK
The Great Purple Hairstreak is wonderful to watch in the sunlight. His stunning wings change color as they turn in the light. Fortunately for butterfly watchers, he is a slow flier and roams most of the United States, from California to New Jersey.

CLOUDED SULPHUR
You can find the Clouded Sulphur in fields and roadsides throughout North America. Swarms of young males often visit mud puddles for a midday drink.

RED ADMIRAL

Not all butterflies are gentle nectar-sippers. Some, like the Red Admiral, are fighters. Although only 2½ inches from wing to wing, the Red Admiral will defend his territory against much larger butterflies and moths. Red Admirals patrol open fields and gardens throughout the United States and southern Canada.

APHRODITE FRITILLARY

The Aphrodite Fritillary is a midsummer butterfly. He doesn't emerge from his chrysalis until late June. Here the Aphrodite is drinking nectar through his long proboscis. When he is not visiting flowers, a butterfly rolls his tongue back up like a fishing line. Aphrodites roam dry fields and brushland from Canada to North Carolina and through most of the Midwest.

PAINTED LADY

Where do butterflies go in the winter? Some survive the cold weather protected in their egg cases or as pupae in their chrysalises. Other hardy types find a sheltered spot and hibernate. But a few put their strong wings to use and fly to warmer places. One frequent flier is the Painted Lady. Throughout the United States, Europe, Africa, and Australia, swarms of Painted Ladies fly hundreds of miles south in the fall and return north in the spring. But as impressive as these journeys are, the Painted Lady is just a commuter compared to the long-distance traveler of the insect world—the Monarch butterfly.

Butterflies from Around the World

From the deep shadows of a rain forest, brilliant wings dart into the sunlight. Like delicate flying blossoms, tropical butterflies appear in a flash of color, then disappear into the foliage. Their beauty is practical, too. The color provides camouflage, and unusual features, like long tails, help to distract an enemy from the butterflies' soft bodies.

BLUE MORPHO

Blue Morphos live in the rain forests of South America. The brownish-red females usually stay in the shadowy underbrush, while the males show off their iridescent wings in open, sunny areas.

ACRAEA BUTTERFLY

Many different kinds of *Acraea* butterflies can be found throughout Africa, from the desert areas to the jungles. The bright red of this *Acraea* is like a stoplight to his enemies, telling them of his bad taste.

TAILED BIRDWING

The Tailed Birdwing is from the remote hilly areas of New Guinea. He spends most of his time flying above the treetops. But in the morning or at dusk, he flies down to visit flowers.

INDIAN LEAF
With folded wings, the Indian Leaf blends into the leaves around him. But if disturbed, he unfolds his wings to show their bright upper sides. This sudden burst of color startles his enemies, and off he flies. The Indian Leaf lives in the forests and along riverbanks in Nepal, Tibet, and southern China.

JEWEL BUTTERFLY
Jewel butterflies keep to the mountains of Central and South America. They are often seen near fruit trees, drinking the juices of the fallen fruit. The round patterns on their wings give them another name, the "figure of eight."

CYTHAERIAS BUTTERFLY
You could stand next to a Cythaerias butterfly and never see him. With his narrow body and transparent wings, the Cythaerias is more than camouflaged—he's invisible! His home is the rain forests of Central and South America.

The Migrating Monarch

For many years, entomologists watched Monarch butterflies begin their fall migration from Canada and the northeastern United States. But where did they go? Huge swarms of Monarchs would head south and vanish somewhere beyond Texas.

In 1976, the winter quarters of the eastern Monarch butterflies was finally found. Beginning in early September, and traveling from twenty to a hundred miles a day, every Monarch in the eastern United States has the same small area in Mexico as its destination. This area, in the Sierra Madre mountains northwest of Mexico City, covers only 2,000 acres. Here an estimated fourteen billion Monarchs cluster so densely that trees 100 feet tall appear to be a solid mass of butterflies.

In March the Monarchs begin to stir. After mating, the butterflies begin to journey north. But this time, the butterflies drift slowly on their way, in small groups or alone. The female stops along the way to lay her eggs on milkweed plants. Soon after, this first generation dies. But their children will hatch, feast on milkweed, and, after emerging from cocoons, continue their parents' journey. The second generation, too, will stop to lay eggs and die off. Only the grandchildren or great-grandchildren of those who made the great migration to Mexico will complete the long journey back.

VICEROY BUTTERFLY

Monarchs love milkweed; it's all they eat. An advantage of their exclusive diet is that it makes them taste terrible. Their awful taste is somehow widely known in the bird kingdom, and birds leave them strictly alone. Their coloring is the opposite of camouflage—it alerts birds to their presence and tells them to look somewhere else for a meal.

The Viceroy butterfly copies the appearance of the Monarch. Scientists call this *mimicry*. Since birds can't tell the difference between the two species, they avoid them both. The colors and design that protect the Monarchs protect the Viceroys, too—plus, they don't have to eat all that milkweed!

Moths and Butterflies

At first glance, butterflies and moths may look much the same to you, but there are ways to tell them apart. First, notice how they hold their wings at rest. A moth holds its wings straight out; a butterfly holds them together, straight up over its body. Then, look at their bodies. Moths are chubbier; butterflies are more slender. Their antennae are different, too. Moths have feathery or hairy antennae, while butterflies have smooth ones with little knobs at the ends. But the easiest way to tell the two apart is by the time of day. If you see a Lepidoptera during the day, it is probably a butterfly. If it is active at night, chances are it is a moth.

Caterpillars and Moths

Most adult moths and butterflies live only a few weeks or days. Their most important job is to find a mate and produce the eggs of the next generation. During this short time, Lepidoptera will eat only enough nectar and pollen to keep up their body weight. But it was a different matter back in their childhood; their most important job then was eating. The larvae of moths can cause great damage to crops and trees.

A good example of a hungry caterpillar is the larva of the Luna moth. As a caterpillar, it eats 8,000 times its own weight in forty-eight hours! Can you imagine the size of a human baby who could do this? All that eating produces the graceful, kite-like adult who roams the night skies of the eastern United States.

Some caterpillars are so well known they outshine their adult forms. Can you guess the childhood identities of these three moths?

SILKWORM

The caterpillar of the pure white moth is the world-famous silkworm, or *Bombyx mori*. Silkworms, who originated in China, are now raised entirely by humans; they no longer live in the wild. When the caterpillars are fully grown, they spin a cocoon out of a single thread of silk. The silk strand from each cocoon can measure a mile and a half in length.

TIGER MOTH

The Tiger moth who visits your porch light was probably better known to you last fall. That's when it was the furry, chubby Woollybear caterpillar. This larva is especially active at the end of summer as it searches for the right spot in which to hibernate. Some people believe the Woollybear can predict the kind of winter we will have. There's a tiny bit of truth to this tale. Caterpillars, as well as other insects, tend to be darker when they are growing during wet weather. At the end of a wet summer, a Woollybear will have very wide black bands. Since a rainy summer may mean a longer winter, very dark Woollybears might forecast a harsh winter.

CHICKWEED MOTH

The pretty yellow-and-pink Chickweed moth can be found throughout the United States. If you can't stay up at night to look for the adult, you can easily see its larval form during the day. It's the familiar inchworm, who arches and stretches its way across leaves.

ATLAS MOTH
The Atlas moth from India and Southeast Asia is one of the largest species of moths. From wing to wing, he can measure twelve inches. That's as long as this page!

POLYPHEMUS MOTH
Like many moths and butterflies, the Polyphemus moth has "eyespots" on her wings that look like the eyes of owls. Since owls are hunters, this is enough to scare most birds right away. Polyphemus moths are found throughout the United States and southern Canada.

SHEEP MOTH

Unlike most moths, the Sheep moth flies during the day. And with wings like a stained-glass window, she's a match for any butterfly. You can find the Sheep moth in mountain meadows from California to the Rockies.

ENDANGERED MOTHS

Butterflies and moths are delicate creatures. Today, their numbers and variety face human threats. Harmless species as well as pests are destroyed by pesticides. A single spraying of pesticide can wipe out twenty generations of moths. Lepidoptera are also endangered by ever-increasing land development, which destroys their favorite food sources. Many larvae are fussy eaters and cannot survive without a few specific plants or trees. Others are endangered by their own beauty and rarity, as collectors attempt to seize the few who remain. Here are just two of the many endangered moths.

The Spanish Moon moth, one of the world's most beautiful creatures, lives in the pine forests of the Pyrenees and the French Alps. It is now protected in Europe.

The Prairie Sphinx, one of the rarest moths in the United States, has had many close calls with extinction. For many years, it was thought to be gone. After its rediscovery in Colorado in 1979, it was nearly killed off by pesticides. A few pupae survived, and the adults made a small comeback. Then, the Prairie Sphinx, along with the small primrose on which it feeds, was attacked by a rival Sphinx moth. Recently, the Prairie Sphinx has struggled back, but its future is uncertain. Collectors, attracted by their scarcity, may destroy those still in existence.

MOSQUITOES

The buzzing of a mosquito is one of the most annoying sounds in nature. If we fail to search and swat, the result is usually just a painful welt. In the tropics, however, the bite can be fatal. Mosquitoes are carriers of yellow fever and malaria, two diseases that still kill thousands of people every year. Even in the northern United States, mosquitoes have caused outbreaks of encephalitis, a deadly disease.

The mosquito's buzzing is produced by a pair of wings that beat with astonishing speed—1,000 times a second! Mosquitoes listen to their sounds as closely as we do, not to ward off a bite but to locate a mate.

Female mosquitoes, the only ones who bite, lay their eggs in water. The larvae, called *wigglers*, develop in the water. In their pupal stage they are called *tumblers*. Like their cousins, the flies, they grow very rapidly. From egg to pupa to annoying adulthood takes only ten days.

FLEAS

This tiny insect has caused more human deaths than all the wars ever fought. It is the Oriental rat flea, the carrier of bubonic plague. These fleas lived on rats, who at one time were very common in households, and infected humans through their bites. During terrible outbreaks from 541 to 1352 A.D., as much as one fourth the population of Europe died from the plague. In all, this disease, also known as the Black Plague, has killed 200 million people in Europe, Africa, and Asia. Today, the plague is treatable with antibiotics, although small outbreaks still occur throughout the world.

You are more likely to encounter the common dog and cat fleas. Like all fleas, they are tremendous leapers. Millions of years ago, fleas may have been fliers; but since wings are easily tangled in fur, wingless jumpers developed. Modern fleas are so tiny that a line of twenty-five would equal one inch, yet they have no trouble traveling. They can easily do high jumps of eight inches and amazing long jumps of twelve inches.

A World Without Insects?

Did you ever wonder, just after you've been bitten by a mosquito or stung by a bee, why we have to have insects at all? Unfortunately, many insects that catch our attention are the pests, or nuisance insects. They eat our crops, interrupt our picnics, and drive us behind screens at night.

If insects disappeared, they wouldn't go alone, for insects are food for many other creatures. Without insects we would have no birds, nor freshwater fish like trout, bass, and salmon. Our gardens and orchards would vanish, too, for just as insects need flowering plants for nectar and pollen, the plants need the insects to carry that pollen from male to female plants. And what a mess our forests would be! Insects such as termites act as decomposers. They break down large pieces of wood so that bacteria and fungi can eat the small pieces. Scavenger insects, like the Bolitotherus beetle and outdoor cockroaches, also help clean up by eating dead and decaying material.

Without insects you could say good-bye to many everyday products. Moths give us silk, bees give us honey, and scale insects provide us with a sticky substance from which shellac is made. Medical research would also suffer without insects. Because they reproduce so quickly, scientists can study many generations in a very short time. The fruit fly, used for research in genetics, is just one example.

As you can see, the work of insects is serious business. But for us, their audience, watching their curious habits and admiring their beauty and variety isn't work at all—it's just fun!